Butch

Miss Loopy

FEB   2004

poochie-poo

Poochie-Poo

Helen Stephens

David Fickling Books

OXFORD · NEW YORK

Thankyou to David (person),
Maria (person), Ness (person)
and Victor (pooch).

A DAVID FICKLING BOOK

Published by David Fickling Books
an imprint of Random House Children's Books
a division of Random House, Inc.
1540 Broadway
New York, New York 10036

Published simultaneously in Canada by Random House of Canada Limited, Toronto. Originally published in Great Britain by David Fickling Books, an imprint of Random House Children's Books.

www.randomhouse.com/kids

Library of Congress Cataloging-in-Publication Data available upon request

ISBN 0-385-75012-9 (trade)—ISBN 0-385-75018-8 (lib. bdg.)

Printed in Singapore

July 2003

10 9 8 7 6 5 4 3 2 1

First American Edition

Victor is a well-behaved, lovable pup and he lives with *Miss Loopy.*

Miss Loopy adores **Victor**. She kisses him and cuddles him whenever she can. She buys him treats, and her favorite thing is to tickle him under his chin and say "Coo-chi-coo!" **Victor** loves being tickled and fussed over except . . .

. . . when his friend **Butch** comes to visit. **Butch** is a very small, very naughty pup. **Victor** thinks **Butch** is cool.

One day **Butch** came to visit. "You two pups play nicely," said *Miss Loopy*. "I'm not playing nicely," said **Butch**. "Let's play baddies." "Yes," said **Victor**. "Let's play baddies."

"Here are some doggy biscuits, you two pups," said *Miss Loopy*. "Delicious!" said **Victor**.

"Baddies don't eat doggy biscuits," said **Butch**. "They eat table legs!"

" Fetch my slippers, darling," said *Miss Loopy.* "Baddies don't fetch slippers," said **Butch**, "they hide them!"

"Good boy, coo-chi-coo!" said *Miss Loopy* and she tickled **Victor's** tummy.

"Baddies don't have their tummies tickled," said **Butch**, "they are too busy stealing sausages!"

"And another thing," said **Butch**, "Baddies aren't called **Victor**. They have names like Buster or Knuckles. You're a useless baddie!"

Victor felt very sad. He tried to think of a way to show **Butch** what a brilliant baddie he was.

No dogs allowed

Later that afternoon, when
Miss Loopy took them shopping,
Victor saw a sign that said:

"NO DOGS ALLOWED."
This gave **Victor** an idea . . .
and he told **Butch**.

"Watch this!" said **Victor**. "I'm going to run into that shop where it says "NO DOGS ALLOWED."

Butch was very impressed.
Victor ran into the shop . . .

. . .then straight back out again! He felt terrible for being so naughty so he shouted to the shopkeeper, "Sorry about that!" "Baddies don't say sorry," said **Butch** and he laughed at **Victor** all the way home.

But **Victor** didn't care
because he didn't want
to be a baddie now.
"I wasn't cut out
for a life of crime,"
he said.

Suddenly the door bell rang. *Miss Loopy* opened the door and there stood *Miss Froopy-Frou-Frou.* "Hello, *Miss Froopy-Frou-Frou,*" said *Miss Loopy.* "Come in."

"Where is my darling pup?"
cried *Miss Froopy-Frou-Frou*.
"Come to Mummikins,
my little poochie-poo.
Have you missed me?
Come on, poochie-poochie-
poochie-poo!"
And *Miss Froopy-Frou-Frou*
picked up **Butch** and
tickled his tummy.

Butch blushed.

"Baddies don't blush!"
said **Victor**.

"Bye, bye," said
Miss Froopy-Frou-Frou.
"Bye, bye,"
called *Miss*
Loopy.

"Bye, bye,
Poochie-poochie-
poochie-poo!"
said **Victor**.

Miss Froopy-Frou-Fro

Butch

Victor

FATHERS DAY
1998

You're The Tops, Pops!

by

SCHULZ

HarperCollins*Publishers*

A Chip
Off The
Ol' Block

HE UNDERSTANDS.. HE SAID WHEN HE WAS LITTLE, HE HID UNDER THE BED FOR THREE DAYS..

Thinking
Of You

I am still living here on the desert as you can see by this post card. I have a lot of friends among the coyotes and cactus.

Snoopy and I see each other once in awhile. He has a good home with a round-headed kid.

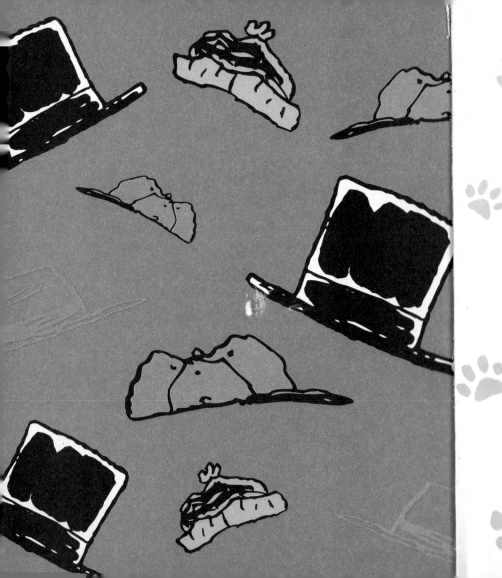

P.S. If you really want to, you can worry about me.

Produced by Jennifer Barry Design, Sausalito, CA
Creative consultation by Kristen Schilo
First published 1998 by HarperCollins*Publishers* Inc.
http://www.harpercollins.com

Based on the PEANUTS ® comic strip by Charles M. Schulz
http://www.unitedmedia.com

ISBN 0-06-757447-5

Printed in Hong Kong

1 3 5 7 9 10 8 6 4 2

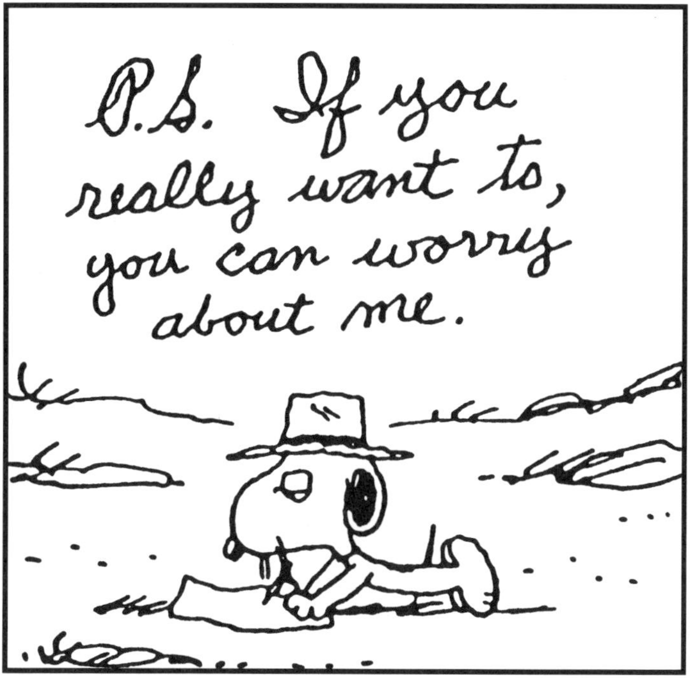

Produced by Jennifer Barry Design, Sausalito, CA
Creative consultation by Kristen Schilo
First published 1998 by HarperCollins*Publishers* Inc.
http://www.harpercollins.com

ISBN 0-06-757447-5

Printed in Hong Kong

1 3 5 7 9 10 8 6 4 2

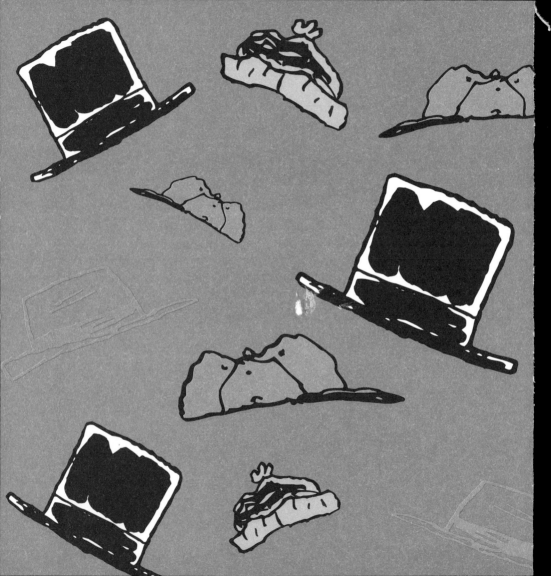